The First Bear in Africa!

The First Bear in Africa!

SATOMI ICHIKAWA

SCHOLASTIC INC

New York   Toronto   London   Auckland   Sydney
Mexico City   New Delhi   Hong Kong   Buenos Aires

My name is Meto. Here is the house where I live with my family and our animals, in a very small village in the middle of the African savanna.

This morning, I hear the noise of a motorcar coming toward us. "Father, Father!" I say. "We are going to have visitors!"

It is a family of tourists who have come to say hello to us!

They must have come from far, far away.

They don't speak our language.

They wear so many clothes!

And they watch us all the time from behind their photographic machines.

I smile. They look funny.

"Meto, show your goat to the little girl," says my father. "It looks like she loves animals, too."

It is true, the little girl also holds an animal in her arms. It is very small, and it has a bright red ribbon around its neck, just like the one the little girl has in her hair.

I have never seen this kind of animal before—it is not from our savanna.

After a very short visit, the family has to go. I feel
sad they are leaving.

"Good-bye," they yell to us from their car.
"*Kwaheri*," we call back to them. Good-bye.

But no! The girl has forgotten her little animal!

"Wait!" I call and I run after her.
"Wait!" I have to catch up with them.

I take a shortcut by the marshes.

"Hello, Meto!" *Kiboko*, a hippopotamus, calls to me. "What are you carrying in your arms? It looks like a beautiful little creature—let me have it for my son!"

"Oh, no, Kiboko!" I yell back. I do not stop to explain.

A little farther away, *Simba*, a lion, is taking a nap with her family. I must be very quiet. I tiptoe.

"Wait!" Simba roars. "I smell a strange smell. Is there a new animal in my kingdom?"

I have no time to answer. The car is getting farther and farther away.

"Hello, *Tembo*!" An elephant! "You have big ears—can you hear the car?"

"Yes, Meto. But I also hear a young girl crying." Tembo points his long trunk to show the way.

"I must find her to give her little animal back to her."

"I have never seen anything like this animal," Tembo says.

"It comes from a country far, far away. It has to go back with that little girl."

"Run, Meto! Quick! If I can hear her, she must still be close by!"

"Hello, *Twiga*." A giraffe. "With your long neck, could you tell me if you see a green car?"

"Yes, I see it," the giraffe says. "It is getting close to a giant bird."

"That must be the plane that will take them back home! Help me, Twiga. I must give this little animal to the girl!"

"How peculiar the animal is! I have never seen a tourist like this one before. Come on, Meto. Climb on my back!"

Twiga gallops, moving his long legs with all his might.
"Wait for us!" Kiboko, Simba, and Tembo shout from behind.
"We want to find out who this strange animal is, too!"

"Faster, Twiga! Faster!" I shout.
"They are leaving!"

"My bear! My bear!" the girl cries.

Bear! That must be the name of the little animal!

"You have found him!" she says. She gives me her red ribbon. "For your goat," she says, and runs back to the plane.

Soon the airplane carrying the little girl and
her animal disappears into the clouds.

The news spreads quickly through the savanna.
"That little animal—he was a bear," says a bounding
antelope.

"A bear?" wonders an old zebra. "But there are
no bears in Africa."

"He was here, I promise!" answers a lion cub.
"The first bear in all of Africa."

"How extraordinary!" they all marvel.

To Rafi

ISBN 0-439-37601-7

Copyright © 1998 by Satomi Ichikawa.
English translation copyright © 2001 by Satomi Ichikawa.
First published in France in 1998 by l'école de loisirs, Paris.
All rights reserved.
Published by Scholastic Inc., 555 Broadway, New York, NY 10012,
by arrangement with Philomel Books, an imprint of Penguin Putnam Books for Young Readers,
a division of Penguin Putnam Inc.
SCHOLASTIC and associated logos are trademarks and/or registered
trademarks of Scholastic Inc.

12 11 10 9 8 7 6 5 4 3 2   2 3 4 5 6 7/0

Printed in the U.S.A.   24

First Scholastic printing, February 2002

Book design by Gunta Alexander

The text is set in Maiandra.

GLOSSARY OF SWAHILI WORDS

Kwaheri: Good-bye

Kiboko: Hippopotamus

Simba: Lion

Tembo: Elephant

Twiga: Giraffe